THE MARK THAT LED ME TO YOU

BOUND BY FATE, CONNECTED BY DESTINY

SHEPHALI HAZRA

I dedicate this book to my Jagannath, my Dadu and Didu, my chhoto Didu, both my fathers (Alok Ranjan Hazra, Deepak kr. Hazra), both my mothers (Susmita Hazra, Soma Hazra), all my siblings (Shivani Hazra, Shubham Hazra, Shivangi Hazra) and nonetheless my Fluffy!

Contents

Foreword

Every story begins with a question.

For me, it was a simple yet profound one: How do we find meaning in the mysteries of life? This book was born from that curiosity, a deep fascination with the unseen connections that guide us, the moments that feel destined, and the symbols that seem to lead us toward something greater than ourselves.

Mystery and spirituality have always intrigued me, and in The Mark That Led Me to You, I've woven both into a journey of discovery—one that goes beyond solving puzzles and instead asks the reader to look within. It is a story of fate, hidden truths, and the choices that shape us.

Writing this book has been a journey in itself—one filled with inspiration, learning, and self-reflection. I hope that as you turn these pages, you too embark on a journey of your own, finding pieces of yourself within the story.

Thank you for allowing me to share this with you. I invite you to step into this world, follow the mark, and see where it leads you.

Shephali Hazra

Preface

Stories have a way of finding us, just as much as we find them. The Mark That Led Me to You was not just something I created—it was something that unfolded before me, piece by piece, like a puzzle waiting to be solved.

I have always been drawn to mystery, not just in books but in life itself. The way small, seemingly insignificant moments can connect to something greater has always fascinated me. The blend of fate, symbols, and the unseen forces that shape our paths inspired me to write this novel. This book is more than just a story—it is an exploration of the unknown, of destiny, and of the quiet signs that often go unnoticed.

While writing this, I found myself questioning how much of our journey is choice and how much is already written. The characters in this book embark on their own search for truth, and through them, I hope readers will reflect on their own paths, their own marks left by time and experience.

This book is my way of bringing together everything that has ever intrigued me—mystery, spirituality, self-discovery—and sharing it with you. I hope it speaks to you in ways beyond just words on a page.

With gratitude,
Shephali Hazra

Acknowledgements

Writing The Mark That Led Me to You has been an incredible journey, and I could not have done it alone.

First and foremost, I want to express my deepest gratitude to **my family** for their unwavering support, patience, and belief in my dreams. Your encouragement has been my greatest strength, and I am forever grateful for your love.

To my **teachers and mentors**, thank you for shaping my understanding of literature and storytelling. Your guidance has played a crucial role in my journey as a writer, and this book would not have been possible without the lessons you imparted.

To **Neelu**, who listened to my endless ideas, gave me feedback, and stood by me through every phase of this journey—thank you for your kindness and constant motivation. Your faith in me kept me going even when I doubted myself.

A special thank you to **Amal K. H.** for giving an identity to my character and being extremely supportive, who has inspired me, knowingly or unknowingly. Whether through a conversation, a shared thought, or a passing moment, you have contributed to the essence of this book in ways I cannot fully express.

Finally, to **my readers**—this book is for you. Thank you for choosing to embark on this journey with me. I hope these pages bring you as much joy, wonder, and reflection as they brought me while writing them.

With gratitude,
Shephali Hazra

Prologue

The mark was always there.

Faint, almost unnoticeable—etched into the old stone, hidden beneath layers of dust and time. Most would walk past it without a second glance. But not **Nirmal**. The moment their fingers traced its shape, something stirred within them. A whisper of familiarity. A feeling they couldn't quite explain.

It wasn't just a symbol. It was a message. A door waiting to be opened.

Somewhere in the distance, the wind howled through the trees, carrying secrets from the past. The air felt heavy, charged with an energy that sent a shiver down their spine. Was it coincidence that they had found this mark? Or had it been waiting for them all along?

As the last rays of sunlight faded, they stepped closer, heart pounding. A choice stood before them—walk away and forget, or follow the unknown.

And some mysteries, once uncovered, can never be ignored.

CHAPTER ONE

The truth stood before me—undeniable, unshakable. And for the first time, I saw myself clearly. No pretences. No illusions. Just *me*. And yet, I had spent so much of my life searching—searching for meaning, for purpose, for something *bigger* than myself. I had always assumed that the answers lay somewhere out there, just beyond my reach. But now, standing on the edge of realisation, reality whispered back, *"You are everything you've been searching for."*

How did I even get here?

For years, I believed my life was nothing more than a series of ordinary, predictable days. A steady nine-to-five job, a simple routine, responsibilities that anchored me to the present. My world was small, structured, familiar. Safe. Or at least, that's what I had always thought. But now—now, that certainty was slipping through my fingers like grains of sand.

Lying in bed, I stared at the ceiling, my thoughts a chaotic storm. I had been looking forward to this weekend, determined to uncover whatever had been gnawing at me for months. And yet, here I was, tangled in a mess of questions with no clear answers.

A sigh escaped my lips.

Not now.

This wasn't something I could solve in a single night. I had already promised myself I would confront it—this weekend.

This weekend...

Something felt off.

My gaze flicked to the alarm clock beside my bed, its red digits glaring at me like an accusation.

6:30 AM.

Panic struck.

Wasn't today a weekday?

The realisation hit me like a slap. My heart pounded as I shot upright, sleep evaporating in an instant. My body moved on autopilot—scrambling out of bed, shoving aside tangled bed-sheets, making a beeline for the bathroom. I reached for the door handle just as a knock sounded on the other side.

I froze.

Amma.

With a hurried breath, I turned back and opened the door. She stood there, her warm eyes twinkling with gentle amusement.

"It's the weekend, Makan."

The words hung in the air for a second longer than necessary.

I blinked.

The weekend?

A mix of confusion and sheer exasperation washed over me.

"Oh, right! Of course. Thanks, Amma. I guess I was just... a little too tired. Heavy weekdays, you know." I forced a laugh, hoping it would mask my embarrassment.

Her knowing smile didn't waver. *"I know you've been working hard lately. Get some rest—I'll wake you up later.*

You've been planning this trip for ages! Let me know when you're heading out, and I'll have your lunch ready."

And just like that, reality clicked back into place.

This was the weekend.

The one I had been counting down to for weeks.

A slow, electric thrill coursed through me.

This was it. The getaway I so desperately needed.

No more waiting. No more second-guessing.

I **needed** to go.

With renewed energy, I rushed to the bathroom, splashed cold water on my face, and pulled myself together. In minutes, I packed my bag, bid a swift farewell to Amma and Appa, and swung my leg over my bike. The engine rumbled beneath me, a steady purr against the quiet morning air.

Gripping the handlebars, I let the moment settle.

This wasn't just another weekend trip.

I was stepping into something unknown—something that had lived only in the corners of my mind until now.

The road stretched ahead, long and winding, disappearing into the horizon. With every passing mile, excitement pulsed through my veins, my heart pounding at the sheer anticipation of stepping into a world that had been calling out to me for far too long.

And after hours of riding, I arrived at **Eravikulam National Park.**

Why here, of all places?

You must be wondering that, right?

But the heart never gives a clear reason. It just pulls you forward, whispering in ways the mind can't comprehend.

And sometimes, you just have to follow.

By then, daylight had faded, and the sun dipped below the horizon, casting the sky in streaks of deep orange and violet. Darkness unfurled across the landscape, blanketing everything in eerie silence.

I slowed my bike to a halt, my pulse quickening as thoughts rushed in.

"What if the guard spots me?"

"What if this is all just a figment of my imagination?"

"Am I making a complete fool of myself?"

I inhaled sharply, willing the doubts away. But one question clung to me, refusing to let go.

"Am I alone in this? Or is someone else caught up in it too?"

For a long moment, I hesitated.

Then, I shook my head.

No.

If I backed out now, I would regret it for the rest of my life.

So, I **chose courage over hesitation.**

Keeping my movements careful, I steered the bike forward, deeper into the unknown. The engine hummed in the silence, low and steady—like the growl of a lion lurking in the night.

Eventually, I reached a secluded valley, hidden from the curious eyes of the world. There was something about this place—something *warm, inviting.*

It felt as though it had been waiting for me.

Exhaustion pressed against me, but my mind refused to rest. Lying on the grass, I let my gaze drift towards the stars. Endless, infinite. My thoughts swirled just as wildly, colliding and scattering into the darkness.

And then—my stomach growled.

I had not eaten all day.

Reaching into my bag, I pulled out the lunch Amma had packed. I took a bite, barely aware of the taste. But then—

Something caught my eye.
Something... breathtaking.
I froze, mid-chew, my heart hammering as I stared at
the sight before me.
And in that moment, I knew—
This was just the beginning.

CHAPTER TWO

As I took a bite of my lunch, my gaze drifted upwards—and in that instant, the world around me ceased to exist.

Above me stretched a celestial masterpiece, a sky so breathtakingly vast and infinite that it made everything else felt completely insignificant. The stars weren't just scattered; they were aligned in a pattern so mesmerizing that it felt like a message, a hidden code waiting to be deciphered. A shiver ran down my spine. *Was this real? Was I dreaming?*

I nudged myself, pinched my arm, even clenched my fists—anything to confirm I hadn't already drifted into sleep. But the chill in the night air, the soft rustling of the wind, and the faint scent of the earth beneath me all told me one thing—*I was very much awake.*

"I am in my senses! I am wide awake!" I reassured myself, yet my own voice sounded distant, as if it belonged to someone else.

The half-eaten bite of food slipped from my fingers, forgotten. My entire being was entranced, locked onto the divine spectacle unfolding before me. I had no control over my body anymore—I was frozen, mesmerized, consumed by something far greater than myself. And then, without thought, without intention, words I had never spoken before flowed from my lips:

"Jagajjalapalam kachad kantha-malam
Sarath-chandrabhalam maha-daitya-kalam
Nabho-neelakayam durava-ramayam
Supadma-sahayam bhaje-ham bhaje-ham."
The chant spilled out of me like an ancient memory resurfacing from the depths of time. It wasn't just words—it was a calling, a plea, a longing that had always existed within me, waiting for this very moment.
"Where are you, my Supadma, my Mahalakshmi?
Where are you?"
My voice trembled, barely a whisper, but in the silence of the valley, it echoed like a forgotten prayer carried by the wind. My heart pounded violently against my chest as an overwhelming sense of déjà vu engulfed me. It was as if I had been here before, as if I had uttered these very words in another lifetime.

And for the first time in my life, I felt something stir deep within me—a force, a presence, an awakening.

Tears of anguish streamed down my face as I clutched my heart, overcome by an indescribable ache. At that very moment, a sharp pain shot through my left arm. As I lifted it, I saw a mark—an 'S'—slowly imprinting itself onto my skin. I went blank, unaware of when my vision began to blur. The next moment, everything faded into darkness.

Suddenly, I felt the warmth of the morning sun gently caressing my face, stirring me from my slumber. My eyes fluttered open in an instant, as if awakened by an unseen force—*as if it were my Supadma's touch.* A deep breath filled my lungs, the crisp mountain air laced with the scent of damp earth and wildflowers.

For a moment, I just lay there, my mind hazy, caught between the dreamlike trance of the night before and the reality of the present. The faint whisper of my plea still clung to the air, lingering in the depths of my mind.

"Is this where destiny has led me?"

"What does this 'S' mean?"

"Where will I find my Supadma?"

The questions circled in my thoughts, unanswered, yet pressing. A strange restlessness crept into me, as though something had shifted within, something I couldn't quite grasp yet.

I sat up and reached for my phone, squinting at the brightness of the screen—**8:30 A.M.**

"Damn! I overslept!" I cursed under my breath, jolted back to the present. Time had slipped through my fingers like sand, and I had lingered here longer than I intended.

Brushing off the grass clinging to my clothes, I grabbed my bag and slung it over my shoulder. The stillness of the valley, once so inviting, now felt eerie, as if it had silently witnessed something I wasn't meant to understand. A sudden urgency filled me—I needed to leave.

Swinging onto my bike, I kick-started the engine, its familiar roar grounding me back into reality. With no clear destination in mind, I simply rode, letting the road decide for me. The morning breeze hit my face, and for a while, I let it wash away the lingering thoughts from the night before.

A few miles down, the aroma of freshly fried snacks and chai pulled me toward a roadside food stall. My stomach growled in protest, reminding me that I hadn't eaten since yesterday. Parking my bike, I ordered a plate of steaming hot vada and a glass of chai, letting the warmth seep into my cold fingers.

As I took my first sip, a thought struck me—*Was I truly lost, or was I being led somewhere?*

With no answers, only more questions, I finished my breakfast, wiped my hands on my jeans, and got back on my bike.

I had no clue where I was headed.

But something inside me whispered—I was meant to find out.

I started replaying everything in my head—every fleeting moment, every sign. Riding into the forest, witnessing that divine constellation, feeling the mysterious 'S' mark burn into my skin like an unspoken prophecy.

What now?

Lost in thought, my bike screeched to a halt as something small darted across my path. My heart lurched. A tiny puppy, no more than a few weeks old, stood trembling in front of my front wheel.

Instinctively, I stepped off my bike, moving cautiously toward it. "Hey there, little one," I murmured, crouching down, extending my hand. But instead of coming closer, the puppy took a few hesitant steps back, its deep, dark eyes locked onto mine.

Something felt... off.

It wasn't fear I saw in those eyes. No, this little creature wasn't frightened of me—it was *calling* me, urging me forward.

A strange pull took hold of me. Without a second thought, I followed.

The puppy padded ahead, weaving through trees and thick undergrowth, glancing back every now and then as if to make sure I was still behind it. *Where are you taking me?* I wondered, stepping carefully over fallen branches and damp leaves.

Then, just as suddenly as it had appeared—it was gone.

I froze, spinning around. *Where did it go?* The forest was completely silent. The rustling of leaves, the distant chirping of birds—everything had vanished into an unsettling stillness.

Panic gripped me. Had I imagined it? *No, I was paying attention the entire time!* But the puppy had disappeared, as if it had never existed at all.

And that's when I saw it.

My breath caught in my throat. My legs felt rooted to the ground as my gaze locked onto the scene before me.

A valley stretched out ahead—vast, untouched, almost sacred. My pulse pounded in my ears as recognition struck me like a thunderbolt.

"*No way...*" I whispered, my voice barely audible.

I had seen this place before. Not in reality, but in my dreams.

The very same valley that had haunted my nights for weeks—the one that had called out to me in visions, stirring something ancient within my soul.

And in those dreams... *I was never alone.*

Someone had always been there with me. A presence, a shadow, a whisper of someone just beyond reach.

My gaze swept across the valley, my chest tightening with anticipation. Was this it? Was this 'S' a clue, leading me to something—or **someone**—I was meant to find?

A sudden gust of wind blew through the trees, as if the universe itself was answering me.

I had no idea what lay ahead.

But I knew one thing for certain—this was only the beginning.

Endless questions with no answers—I was exhausted from it all.

When would this finally end? Where was this journey leading me? Was I even on the right path?

It felt as if I were living two lives—one rooted in reality, the other tangled in something beyond my comprehension. But which one was truly mine? Or worse... what if neither was real?

I clenched my fists, frustration bubbling inside me. I needed to know.

Everything.

The truth, the meaning behind the 'S,' the reason why I had been pulled into this strange, inexplicable journey. My past, my future—my entire self—hinged on finding the answers. And for that, I needed my 'S'... the key to it all.

Taking a deep breath, I pulled out my phone and snapped a picture of the valley, capturing the eerie beauty that had drawn me here. Proof that this moment existed, that I wasn't losing my mind.

With a heavy heart, I turned to leave. But the moment my foot shifted, I froze.

My breath hitched. My pulse thundered in my ears.

Right in front of me stood Poppy.

I blinked, my brain struggling to process what I was seeing.

No... it couldn't be.

But there he was. My baby. My Poppy.

The very same Poppy I had lost two years ago—gone too soon, taken from me by a mysterious heart condition no vet could explain. I had grieved him, mourned him, said my goodbyes. And yet, here he was.

Those sparkling eyes, that wagging tail, the same playful yet mischievous look that only he had.

My throat tightened, emotions crashing into me all at once.

I wasn't imagining this.

I knew my Poppy better than I knew myself.

This was him.

But how?

I reached forward, desperate to hold him, to feel his warmth one more time. But before my fingertips could even graze his fur—he was gone.

Vanished.

Like mist dissolving into the morning air.

A hollow silence swallowed the forest around me, amplifying the emptiness left in his absence. My heart clenched, shattering into countless pieces. I could feel the sting of my own pulse, the unbearable ache spreading through my chest like wildfire.

Tears welled up, blurring my vision, but I made no effort to wipe them away. My legs gave out beneath me, and I sank to the ground, defeated.

That little puppy... it was Poppy.

My Poppy.

He had found me again. Guiding me, just as he always did whenever I was lost.

But why? Why now? What was he trying to tell me?

I wanted to scream, to demand answers from the universe, but all that escaped from within me was a choked sob. The pain of losing him once had nearly broken me—now, losing him yet again, in a way I couldn't even comprehend, was unbearable.

I sat there, motionless. Minutes passed. Then an hour. Then two.

The world around me continued as if nothing had happened. The wind rustled through the trees. Birds called out in the distance. But inside me, time had stopped. I sat like a stone—shocked, sobbing, and above all, broken.

I was drowning in my own tears—tears of grief, exhaustion, and something even deeper... something I couldn't quite name.

And then, amidst the overwhelming heartache, a single thought surfaced, cutting through the fog of my mind like a whisper from the unknown:

Was Poppy a part of this too?

Had he been sent to lead me to something? Or someone?

The weight of it all pressed down on me, suffocating, relentless. And in the depths of my sorrow, one question echoed louder than all the rest—

Why me?

I gathered every ounce of courage and forced myself to my feet, though my legs felt weak, and my heart weighed heavier than ever. My swollen eyes still carried the remnants of my tears, a silent testament to everything I had just endured.

Somehow, I reached my bike, gripping the handles tightly as if holding onto the last fragments of my sanity. With a deep sigh, I started the engine—this time, more cautious, more aware. The sound of the motor filled the silence around me, yet my mind remained trapped in an endless loop, replaying everything that had happened.

Poppy. The valley. The mysterious 'S'.

Was I closer to the truth, or just sinking deeper into a void I wasn't prepared for?

The thought lingered as I rode back home, my mind settling on an unknown conclusion—one I couldn't fully grasp yet.

By the time I reached home, the sun was dipping below the horizon, casting long shadows across our doorstep. Amma stood at the entrance, waiting, her eyes instantly scanning my face the moment I stepped inside.

Her gaze softened with concern. "Did you cry?"

My breath hitched. She knew. She always did.

But I wasn't ready to tell her. Not yet.

I forced a weak smile, shaking my head. "No, Amma. I just fell asleep for a while. Must've woken up with a puffy face, that's all."

She didn't believe me. I could see it in her eyes. But she let it slide, choosing to trust that I would tell her when I was ready. That was Amma—never forcing, always knowing.

Muttering something about being tired, I excused myself and went straight to my room. The moment I shut the door behind me, I felt the exhaustion crash over me like a tidal wave.

I collapsed onto my bed, staring blankly at the ceiling, feeling puzzled, heartbroken, and drained all at once.

I had embarked on this journey searching for answers.

But now, I wasn't sure if I was even ready to face them anymore.

CHAPTER FOUR

I kept staring at the wall, my mind blank, my body still. Then, out of nowhere, I saw something—or someone.

There stood my Poppy, just a few feet away, his tail wagging, his eyes glistening with the same warmth I had always known. But he wasn't alone. Beside him was a woman. No—not just any woman. A young lady, possibly in her early twenties, draped in an ethereal glow. She wasn't fully there, her form flickering like a candle in the wind, a faint presence lingering in my room.

My breath caught in my throat. Who was she?

She stepped closer, her movements slow, deliberate, as if time itself had lost its grip on her. And then, without a word, she reached out—her delicate fingers pressing against the mysterious 'S' mark.

The moment she touched it, the air around me shifted. Everything blurred, twisted, and before I could react, a vision unfolded before my eyes.

I saw myself—but not as I was now.

I was seated at the edge of some divine realm, high above, gazing down upon the world below. There was an unexplainable peace in my heart, a purpose I had never known before. I wasn't lost. I wasn't searching. I was guiding. Helping. Watching over those in need.

A sudden shrill sound tore through the silence.

My phone rang.

I jolted awake, gasping, my chest rising and falling rapidly. Sweat clung to my skin, my hands trembling as I reached for my phone.

I blinked, trying to shake off the haze. "Oh god!" I exhaled sharply, running a hand through my hair. "When did I even drift into such a deep sleep?"

But that wasn't the real question.

The real question was—

What on earth had I just experienced?

The stack of questions kept growing, piling up like an insurmountable mountain, while the answers seemed to drift further and further away, slipping through my fingers like grains of sand. I felt trapped, drowning in a sea of uncertainty, gasping for a way out.

"Is there any way out of this?" I muttered under my breath, my voice barely audible in the stillness of my room. My own words echoed back at me, but they carried no comfort, no solution—just more confusion.

Then, like a sudden flash of lightning slicing through a stormy sky, it hit me—

The 'S'!

I gasped as the mark burned itself into my mind, searing its presence into my thoughts. My pulse quickened, my hands clenched into fists. This had to mean something. It wasn't just a coincidence.

"Is there a way to reach this 'S'?" I whispered, my heart pounding like a war drum in my chest.

My thoughts spiraled, my mind scrambling to make sense of it all. What—or who—was 'S'? Was it a name? A place? A sign? My brain raced through every possibility, desperately trying to recall every name, every memory, every moment tied to the letter 'S.'

And in that desperate search, a chilling realization crept over me—
What if the answer had been in front of me all along?
"Could it be Saachi from school?... Sakshi from work?... Or Sonakshi, my neighbour?..." I murmured, grasping at straws, desperately trying to connect the dots. My mind raced, sifting through memories, searching for any lingering emotion, any forgotten moment that could link me to one of them.
"But no," I muttered to myself, shaking my head. "It couldn't be any of them. If it were, wouldn't I have felt something before? A connection, a sign—anything?"
I exhaled sharply, running a hand through my hair. The shadowy figure I had seen bore no resemblance to any of them. The presence I had felt... It was different. Otherworldly. Familiar yet unknown. It wasn't just a name—it was something far beyond what I could comprehend.
Lost in the depths of my own thoughts, I barely noticed the soft knock at my door until my Amma's voice pulled me back to reality.
"Nirmal," she called gently from outside. "Come out and have some food. Your Appa has been waiting for you. Join us at the table. Come sit with us."
Her voice carried warmth, a quiet plea woven into her words. I blinked, as if waking from a trance, and for the first time in what felt like hours, I was reminded of the real world—the one where I was just Nirmal, a son, a brother, a man who had drifted too far into the unknown.
I stepped out to have my meal, only to be met with a flood of questions from my Amma and Appa—about my trip, my work, and most of all, about me.

"More questions?" I thought to myself, suppressing a sigh. But then came the one question I hadn't prepared for. "How are you, Nirmal?"

I opened my mouth to answer but found myself utterly speechless. How was I? How could I possibly put into words the chaos swirling inside me? How could I explain the strange visions, the inexplicable pull towards an unknown truth, the weight of questions that only seemed to multiply?

And how did they even sense my state of mind? Was it really that obvious?

It felt like an endless loop—questions, more questions, but never an answer.

The silence stretched, and I could feel their eyes on me, waiting, expecting. But I wasn't ready. I wasn't sure if I ever would be.

So, I excused myself, muttering something vague, and hurried away before they could press further. But I could feel it—the unspoken tension settling in the air.

I couldn't meet their eyes. Not because I was ashamed, but because I was afraid. Afraid that if I did, they would see the truth reflected in mine. Afraid that they would dismiss it as nonsense.

I knew I couldn't tell them—or anyone. They'd never believe me.

They'd say I was imagining things. That I was overthinking. They'd tell me to stay quiet, to stop searching, to move on. And if they didn't say it, they'd ignore me completely. And that would hurt even more.

Just like all the other times I was pushed aside. Forgotten.

"I know I'm not the favourite among the three of us, but I can't be that bad, right?" I thought, my own voice uncertain. Was I convincing myself? Seeking validation from within?

I let out a bitter chuckle, shaking my head. It didn't matter.

Because no matter how much I tried to hold onto the world I had built, reality was calling me—and I could feel it pulling me in.

CHAPTER FIVE

I was always the kind one—the one who listened, who understood, who stood by people when they needed someone the most. Empathy and compassion weren't just qualities I possessed; they were the very foundation of my being. I didn't just accept this part of me—I cherished it. There was an odd sense of fulfilment in helping others, in being the person people could rely on. It made me feel like I had a purpose, like I mattered.

But like every coin has two sides, so did I.

For the most part, I was calm, patient—someone who believed in kindness even when it wasn't returned. But there was another side of me, buried deep within, a side so contrasting to my usual self that even I feared it. It rarely surfaced, but when it did, it was like a storm breaking free after years of silent brewing. When provoked beyond my limit, my anger wasn't just a fleeting outburst—it was a force. A wildfire that burned everything in its way. I wasn't reckless, nor was I impulsive. But when pushed to the edge, I didn't believe in turning back.

I wasn't the best person in the world—I had my flaws, my imperfections. But if there was one thing I did understand, it was justice. I lived by two rules: "No Forgiveness" and "Tit-for-Tat."

To me, forgiveness was a privilege, one that not everyone deserved. If someone wronged me, I believed in giving them exactly what they had given me—nothing more, nothing less. I never sought revenge out of spite, but I believed in balance. I believed in karma. And if karma ever needed a helping hand, I was more than willing to be its instrument.

School was never much of a struggle for me. I wasn't the brightest student in the room, but I was good enough—disciplined, hardworking, and smart in my own way. I sailed through those years without much turbulence, blending into the rhythm of classes, exams, and friendships that rarely lasted beyond the classroom walls.

Then came college—a whole new world, filled with unfamiliar faces and unspoken expectations. I pursued Civil Engineering, stepping into a phase of life that was supposed to shape my future. But more than academic lessons, it was life itself that became my greatest teacher.

By the time I made it through those years, I had already seen enough to carve three undeniable truths into my soul:

1. Trust is a fragile thing—handle it with caution.

2. Not everyone who shares your laughter shares your loyalty.

3. In the end, you are your own master.

These lessons weren't taught in a classroom. They weren't part of a syllabus or written in textbooks. They were learned through experience—through trust misplaced, through friendships broken, through moments that left scars deeper than I cared to admit.

During my college years, I decided to give love a chance. Between endless lectures, late-night assignments, and the whirlwind of campus life, I found myself drawn to Priya. She was the kind of girl who could light up a room just by walking in—graceful, soft-spoken, and always carrying a warmth that felt rare in a world full of indifference. She listened when I spoke, laughed at my jokes, and made me believe, for the first time, that I had found someone who truly saw me.

With Priya, everything felt effortless. Love wasn't something I had gone searching for, but with her, it felt natural—like slipping into a rhythm that had always existed, just waiting for the right moment to unfold. She made me feel understood, valued, almost like I was the only person that mattered in her world. And I fell—hard and fast, never once questioning if the feeling was real.

But illusions have a way of shattering when you least expect them to.

Behind the gentle smiles and affectionate words, Priya was nothing like the girl I had come to love. While she held my hand in public, she was busy whispering into the ears of others behind my back. She wove stories—intricate, venomous, and far from the truth. She painted me as someone I was not, twisting words, bending realities, and feeding lies into the world around us.

And the worst part?

I had no clue.

I trusted her. I let my guard down. I gave her pieces of myself I had never shared with anyone, believing she was the one person who wouldn't use them against me. But little did I know, the very hands I held so dearly were the ones weaving the web of my downfall.

It started with small things—strange looks from friends, hushed conversations that ended the moment I walked into a room. I dismissed them at first, thinking it was nothing.

But then, the whispers turned into words, the words into stories, and soon, I realized that I was no longer in control of my own narrative.

People started seeing me through Priya's lens—through the falsehoods she so skillfully crafted. And by the time I understood what was happening, the damage was already done.

I confronted her with a broken heart and a soul drowning in betrayal. My voice trembled, my hands clenched, yet beneath the anger, all I felt was sorrow. I wanted answers—needed them. But when she looked at me with tear-filled eyes, something in me wavered.

She cried, weaving apologies laced with fragile excuses, her words tumbling out in desperate pleas. And the fool that I was—the ever-forgiving, ever-empathetic soul—I gave in.

She swore it was a mistake, swore she never meant to hurt me. Uttering some carefully crafted nonsense, she pulled me back into her web of deception. And despite everything, despite the aching truth clawing at my chest...

I believed her.

Again.

CHAPTER SIX

I convinced myself that she loved me—that whatever lines she had crossed, she would never do it again. I clung on to the belief that she had set her own limits, that this time, she would stay within them. My love for her was beyond explanation, beyond reason, and maybe that was why I couldn't bear to see her cry.

Looking back now, I see it clearly. It wasn't love, not in the way I had convinced myself it was. It was the illusion of love—the desperate hunger to feel chosen, to be seen in a way I had never been before. She filled a void I had never dared to acknowledge, and in my eagerness to hold on to that warmth, I let my heart blind me to the truth.

Perhaps, in her arms, I had found what my parents had never given me—**undivided focus**, the feeling of being chosen, of being *seen*. And so, I let my heart override my mind. I ignored the warning signs, silenced my doubts, and held on to this blank belief that she was the one for me.

Because for the first time in my life, I felt like I mattered. And I wasn't ready to let that go.

Soon, I realized that all those tears—all that crying—had been nothing more than a carefully woven trap. She had played with my feelings once again, twisting my emotions like a puppet master pulling invisible strings.

She was the slow poison that seeped into my life, destroying me bit by bit, not with loud betrayals, but with subtle, calculated cruelty.

She accused me of being controlling, of being obsessively possessive, and she did it with such unwavering conviction that even I began to doubt myself. Her words spread like wildfire, whispered into the ears of those I once trusted. When my friends finally approached me, hesitant yet concerned, asking if what she said was true—I didn't even have the strength to respond.

I didn't cry. No tears fell, no words escaped my lips. But something inside me **clicked**. A silent shift, a deep crack forming within. This time, it wasn't just pain—it was something far greater. Far darker.

At first, I tried to fight it, to hold on to fragments of the person I used to be. But Priya was relentless. Slowly, she drained me of all the warmth I once carried, turning my trust into ashes. The person I once was—the carefree, happy soul—was slipping away, and I could do nothing to stop it.

My laughter, my light-heartedness, the warmth I carried within me had all faded into something unrecognizable. It was as if she had reached into my very core and stolen the essence of who I used to be, leaving behind nothing but emptiness.

As if the quiet neglect I had endured at home wasn't enough, she added her own brand of cruelty to the mix. Her betrayal wasn't just a wound—it was a slow poison, seeping into every corner of my being, turning warmth into ice, trust into scepticism.

From that moment on, I was certain—I would never again be the fool who fell so deeply, so blindly, for someone who thrived on deception. No longer would I be an easy target for whispered lies and hollow affections. I would transform, not just into someone stronger, but into someone unshakable. No longer would I place my trust in illusions. No longer would I mistake kindness for weakness. If life had taught me anything, it was that the world didn't reward the naïve—it devoured them. And I was done being prey. I wouldn't merely believe in karma—I would become it, delivering justice with a steadiness that no lie could shake.

I cut all ties with her—completely, irreversibly, and for good. I wanted nothing to do with a woman who had so effortlessly twisted the truth, who spread venomous lies without a second thought. But what baffled me the most wasn't just her deceit—it was her audacity. Did she truly believe people were so blind, so foolish, that they wouldn't eventually see through her web of manipulation?

This time, she didn't even bother shedding her usual fake tears. No desperate apologies, no elaborate justifications. Instead, she laughed—an ugly, hollow sound that sent shivers down my spine. And in that moment, I saw her for what she truly was. No mask, no pretence—just the raw, vicious reality of the person she had always been.

How did I not see this before? How could I have been so blind, so naïve? I mistook my innocence for stupidity, my kindness for weakness. But never again.

CHAPTER SEVEN

Thoughts like these kept me awake, my mind tangled in the remnants of the past, refusing to let go. I turned on my side, staring blankly at the ceiling, trying to shake off the heaviness in my chest. And then, just like that—Poppy.

His tiny, familiar figure surfaced in my thoughts, filling the empty spaces of my heart. I could almost feel his warm presence beside me, his soft fur brushing against my skin.

But the comfort was fleeting. In an instant, the last moments I held him in my arms came rushing back—the weight of his little body, the way his paws rested so trustingly in my hands for the final time.

A lump rose in my throat, and before I could stop it, moisture blurred my vision. I wasn't just remembering him—I was reliving the ache of losing him.

The weight of my thoughts became unbearable, pressing down on me like an invisible force. Loss clung to me—not just Poppy's absence but something deeper, something I couldn't name. I needed air, space—anything to escape the suffocating spiral of emotions.

I glanced at my phone. **1:30 A.M.**

I had work in the morning, the same mundane routine waiting for me. But at that moment, I couldn't care less. I had to get out. The stillness of the night called to me, promising a quiet solace the day never could.

Stepping outside, my eyes fell on my bike and car, parked side by side in their usual spot. A strange sense of familiarity washed over me, as if they weren't just machines but an extension of myself—silent companions, always waiting, always there. There was comfort in their presence, in the way they stood still yet ready, like guardians of my restless soul.

I slid into my car, gripping the wheel without a clear destination in mind. Yet, somehow, my heart already knew where I was headed to.

The Krishna temple near my home.

Why there? I had no definite answer. It wasn't a conscious choice, more like an instinct—an invisible pull toward the one place that had always given me solace. Krishna wasn't just a deity to me; he was my friend, my confidant. From childhood, I had spoken to him the way one would to a trusted companion. My secrets, my fears, my heartbreaks—I had poured them all out before him, never expecting answers, just comfort in his silent presence.

And he never failed me.

He listened without judgment, smiled down at me as if to say, *I am here. You are not alone.* And in that unwavering presence, I found the strength I had always needed.

I would like to share one moment—one undeniable instance—when Krishna, my **Madhumohana**, made his presence known in my little world.

It was the darkest phase of my life. **I had lost two of my greatest companions at once—Poppy, my beloved pet, and the love I had so naively trusted.** The weight of heartbreak pressed down on me, suffocating, relentless. I felt hollow, as if a part of me had been ripped away, leaving behind nothing but an aching emptiness.

With nowhere else to turn, I found myself at **his** doorstep—at the temple, standing before the ever-smiling **Kanha**. I looked up at him, my eyes searching for something—perhaps comfort, perhaps reassurance, or maybe just a sign that I wasn't as alone as I felt.

And then it happened.

Out of nowhere, a little boy came running through the temple doors. He didn't stop, didn't hesitate. He ran straight to me—as if he had been looking for me all along. Without a word, he climbed onto my lap, his tiny fingers gripping mine with a certainty that sent a tremor through my soul. The dam inside me broke.

In that moment, I felt something shift.

The warmth of his small hands seeped into my cold, grieving heart. I could feel my pain unravel, melting away in the innocent embrace of a child who didn't even know me, yet somehow knew exactly what I needed.

I looked back at **Madhumohana**, my Krishna, and in his silent, knowing smile, I understood—this was him. This was his way of reminding me that he was there, always. **And this? This was just one of the many times he came to my rescue.**

As I reached the temple, a wave of disappointment washed over me. **The curtains were drawn, the main entrance locked.** A quiet stillness filled the air, interrupted only by the distant rustling of leaves and the occasional ringing of temple bells in the background.

But I needed him.

I needed my Madhumohana.

Desperation gripped me as I stood there, staring at the closed doors that separated me from the one presence that had always been my solace. **Where are you, Kanha? Please... come to me.**

With a heavy heart, I lowered myself onto the cool marble floor, facing the glass door that led to the sanctum. The pedestal where Krishna's idol stood was hidden behind thick curtains, shielding him from my view. But I knew he was there. **He had to be.** He has always been.

I buried my face in my palms, and the dam I had tried so hard to hold back broke. Silent sobs shook my body as tears spilled freely, my pain pouring out in the only way it knew how. Yet, even as I wept, my gaze remained fixed in his direction, searching, yearning.

And then—through the haze of my tears—a shadow moved. A silhouette, faint yet unmistakable, shifting against the dim glow of temple lights.

It stood near the temple's sanctum, bathed in soft moonlight filtering through the glass. It was **mesmerizingly surreal, almost divine.** My breath hitched, my body frozen in place. **Was it him?** My eyes refused to look away, drawn to the ethereal presence before me.

And then, suddenly—**a gentle tap on my shoulder.**

Startled, I turned around, my pulse quickening.

There he was.

The same little boy. The one who had unknowingly comforted me before, standing before me once again. His innocent eyes held no words, yet they carried an unspoken understanding, as if he had been sent here just for me. Without hesitation, I pulled him close, wrapping him in an embrace as I pressed a kiss to his soft cheek.

"Are you hungry?" I whispered, my voice barely steady.

He didn't say a word.

He simply nodded.

I took his small, warm hand in mine and led him to a nearby 24/7 store. The dim streetlights cast long shadows on the pavement as we walked in silence, his little fingers curled around mine with a trust so pure it made my heart ache.

Once inside, I knelt to his level and asked softly, "**What would you like to have?**"

He looked at me with innocent eyes and replied in a gentle voice, "**Paal.**" Which meant milk in Malayalam.

I smiled, nodding, and picked up milk from the shop. Wanting to make sure he had more than just that, I grabbed a few snacks as well. As I turned to him, handing over the items, he suddenly grasped my hand tighter and whispered,

"**You are soon going to find your 'S'.**"

I froze.

His words sent a strange shiver down my spine, their meaning elusive yet profound. Before I could ask what he meant, he took the snacks from my hands and turned away.

"**Wait—where are you going?**" I called out, stepping forward.

But he didn't answer.

I bolted after him, my pulse racing, but within seconds, he was gone—vanished into the quiet night as if he had never been there.

I felt like a stone, unable to move anymore.

Somehow, I gathered the courage to steady my breath and quickened my steps back toward the temple. My heart pounded, but this time, it wasn't from confusion or fear—it was from an unshakable certainty.

Standing before the temple doors, I closed my eyes and whispered, "**Thank you, Madhumohana.**" A wave of warmth spread through me, as if an unseen presence had wrapped me in reassurance.

I knew exactly what I had to do.

Without hesitation, I got into my car and sped home. The streets were silent, the city asleep, but my mind was wide awake. What felt like an eternity on the road was merely five minutes. As soon as I reached home, I rushed inside, straight to my room, my hands trembling slightly—not with doubt, but with determination.
I picked up my phone, opened Instagram, and typed....

CHAPTER EIGHT

I typed... **Radha**.

The moment my fingers pressed the search button, my breath hitched. My eyes widened in disbelief as the very first account that appeared on my screen belonged to the most breath-taking woman I had ever seen.

Words failed me. **How could I even begin to describe something so surreal? Was she real?** She was mesmerizing, almost ethereal—ravishing, alluring, as if she had stepped right out of my dreams and into reality. My dream woman was right in front of me, yet she felt just out of reach.

I stared at her profile picture, unable to look away. A strange mix of exhilaration and nervousness washed over me. **Should I text her?, What if she doesn't reply?, What if she already had someone in her life?**

But in that moment, every ounce of pain, every burden I had carried, simply vanished. My past no longer held power over me. All that mattered was this pulse-racing, heart-thudding moment.

Summoning every bit of courage I had left, I took a deep breath, let my fingers glide over the keyboard, and typed—

"**Radhey Radhey.**"

And then, I waited.

"**Maybe this isn't the right time,**" I told myself, forcing my phone onto the nightstand. "**She must be asleep... and probably, I should sleep too.**"

But how could I? My mind was spinning, my heart racing, and an electrifying anticipation pulsed through me. I had texted her. **I had actually texted her.**

I lay in bed, staring at the ceiling, my fingers itching to check my phone just one more time. **What if she replies right now? What if she doesn't?** My excitement was almost unbearable. My thoughts swirled until they blended into a blur, and before I knew it, exhaustion won.

Darkness—> Silence—> Sleep.

Then—**knock, knock.**

A sharp knocking on my door jolted me awake. My mom's voice followed, muffled but firm. "**Wake up! It's Monday!**"

I groaned, rubbing the sleep from my eyes, momentarily disoriented. **Monday? Already?** The weekend had slipped away, lost in the whirlwind of emotions.

As soon as she left, I sat up, my mind snapping back to what truly mattered. My hands fumbled for my phone, my heart hammering with an urgency I hadn't felt in ages.

Had she replied?

I unlocked the screen, feeling a rush of excitement unlike anything I had experienced in a long time. **This anticipation, this rush, this sheer thrill—had I forgotten what happiness felt like?**

I stared at her picture once again, completely entranced. **If just an image of this woman could shift my entire mood, what would her presence do to my life?**

A slow smile crept onto my lips. **I was about to find out.**

I tapped on the chat-box, my fingers trembling ever so slightly. There it was. A single notification. My heart pounded. **One message.**

I clicked it open, and there it was—"**Radhey RadheyPrabhuji.**"

For a moment, the world around me ceased to exist. My heart stuttered, skipping beats as if it had forgotten how to function. My mind wiped itself clean, erasing every worry, every doubt, every painful memory. **This was the only moment I wanted to remember.**

She replied. My Radha had replied.

Without wasting a second, I hastily typed back, my excitement barely allowing me to form words. "**You know what? You look exactly like Radha from a painting of Radha-Krishna that I have at my place. Wait, let me send it.**"

I attached the image, my pulse racing. **Would she see what I saw? Would she feel what I was feeling?**

And then, I hit send.

Unwillingly, I placed my phone on the charger, my heart resisting the separation. I didn't want to stop—not yet. But responsibilities called, and as much as I wanted to stay in this moment, I had an office to go to, deadlines to meet, and a life that refused to pause just because my heart had suddenly found a new rhythm.

Dragging myself to the bathroom, I let my thoughts wander—**How do I tell my Radha that she is mine?**

A dozen scenarios played out in my head. Some dramatic, some utterly ridiculous. In one, she had a boyfriend, and I, like a true Bollywood hero, fought him for her, standing victorious in the end. In another, she was already waiting for me, knowing that destiny had led us here.

By the time I snapped out of my daydream, I was already dressed. Without wasting a second, I rushed back to my phone. Had she replied? Had I made her wait too long?

I unlocked the screen, my pulse quickening as I checked the chat. **What if she was thinking about me too?**

And there it was—a reply from her.

I held my breath as I opened the chat. Her message was in Hindi:

"Ye aap kya bol rahe hain? Main aur Maa Radha? Main unke charan raj ke samaan bhi nahi."

(What are you saying? I am nothing like Maa Radha. I can never even be the dust of her feet.)

Her humility struck me like lightning. A simple text, yet it held so much grace, so much depth.

At that moment, clarity washed over me. Until now, I thought what I felt for Priya was love but it was a mere attraction, an infatuation built upon my emotional needs.

But this—this was something else entirely.

I had fallen for her.

It wasn't just the way she looked, but the way she spoke, the way she carried devotion in her words. This wasn't just admiration. **This was love. She was love.**

I was no longer just a man who had stumbled upon a beautiful face on a screen—I was a man with purpose, with conviction.

I wanted her in my life. No, I **needed** her in my life. She wasn't just a dream; she was the kind of reality I had unknowingly longed for.

And Madhumohana—my eternal friend, my silent guardian—had known it all along.

He had led me here, to **her.**

This wasn't coincidence. This was fate.

And now, I was determined to claim the love that was always meant to be mine.

I typed out a message, my fingers hesitating over the keyboard.

I was determined to tell her **everything**—from the very start, every wound, every battle I had fought within myself. But why?

I had never shared my story with anyone before. Not a word. Not a fragment.

Then why did I feel this unexplainable pull toward her? What was it about her that made me want to lay bare my soul, to let her step into the darkest corners of my life?

On what basis was I placing my trust in her? After everything I had been through, after every betrayal, every misplaced faith—why did she feel like the exception?

Logic told me to hold back. But something deeper, something unshakable, whispered otherwise.

She will guard your trust like a sacred vow.

I poured my heart into a long, unfiltered paragraph, my fingers moving rapidly across the keyboard, oblivious to the world around me. Time slipped away unnoticed—minutes turning into moments, lost in the flow of my emotions.

Reality, however, had no patience for my distractions. I had an office to attend, a manager waiting for my report, and a system that demanded my obedience. As much as these routines felt trivial in comparison to what I was experiencing, they still held undeniable power over me.

Because at the end of the day, they came with a pay-check. And like it or not, money had a way of keeping me bound to a life I often wished to escape.

CHAPTER NINE

While waiting for her to read my messages, I hurried through my morning routine, dressing up for the day with a single thought dominating my mind—**her reply**. I wanted to breeze through breakfast, get done with all the mundane tasks, and return to what truly mattered: *our conversation*.

I barely tasted my food, swallowing each bite hastily, eager to be free from the obligations of the morning. Once done, I sank onto the living room sofa, checking the time. There were still a few minutes left before I had to leave for the office. Just enough time.

With anticipation bubbling inside me, I opened our chat, and there it was—a new message from her. A simple string of words, yet it sent a strange power surging through me:

"You don't yet realise what you actually are."

Her words held a depth I couldn't fully grasp, but they made my heart race. What did she mean? And why did it feel like she had just uncovered a truth about me that I hadn't even begun to understand myself? Is she some angel? Or my destiny?

I wanted to ask her everything. I wanted answers to all the questions swirling in my mind, to understand the meaning behind her words. But I held myself back. Rushing wouldn't do any good.

Instead, I let my fingers hover over the keyboard for a moment before settling on something simple—an emoji, a small nervous laugh. It wasn't much, but it was enough to acknowledge her words without demanding too much.

Deep down, though, I knew this conversation was far from over.

But she wasn't just anyone—she was an angel, a soul so kind and pure that I couldn't help but be drawn to her. I hadn't expected her to reply, but she did.

Our conversation flowed effortlessly, and soon, we exchanged names and talked about where we lived. She was from Delhi, and I was from Kerala.

"Amazing," I thought to myself. "A long-distance connection!"

The distance should have felt like an obstacle, but instead, it intrigued me. It made our conversation feel even more special, as if fate had woven an invisible thread between us, tying together two soul miles apart.

I had finally learned my Radha's real name—**Shiuli**. A name as soft and ethereal as the night-blooming jasmine it was meant to embody. Yet, no flower, no matter how delicate, could ever compare to her. She was something else entirely—**radiant, elusive, breathtaking**.

A shiver ran through me.

Shiuli.

Could this be it? Could this be what the 'S' mark was trying to tell me all along? Was it a mere coincidence, or had destiny carved her name into my very skin before I even knew her?

I suddenly glanced at the time—I was going to be late. Without wasting another second, I excused myself and dashed out, hopping onto my bike. The engine roared to life, and I sped through the streets, reaching my office in a record fifteen minutes. I had never ridden this fast before! But even as I weaved through traffic, my mind was lost elsewhere—lost in thoughts of my Radha, my Shiuli. Why and how all of a sudden she appeared in my life just as I got the mark? That mesmerizing face, the way she carried herself with such grace, and the gentleness in her texts—everything about her had taken root in my heart.

I was completely drowning in thoughts of her, lost in the depths of her presence, when suddenly—like a lightning bolt striking my mind—I remembered something!

That silhouette... the one I had seen in my room, standing beside my Poppy. A woman, her presence ethereal, almost divine. My breath hitched as realization washed over me.

It was her.

It had always been her!

The 'S' mark!

Madhumohana had led me to her... my 'S'—my Shiuli! A strange thought crept into my mind, unshakable in its persistence. This wasn't the first time I had encountered an unexplainable sign. As a child, I used to have vivid dreams—dreams of a girl standing beneath a night-blooming jasmine tree, whispering something I could never quite remember upon waking. And now, here she was, **Shiuli**, named after the very flower I had dreamt of.

I suddenly recalled an old diary tucked away in my childhood home. It had belonged to my grandfather, who often spoke of the soul's eternal journey. I had never paid much attention to his words back then, but a sudden urge struck me—what if there was something inside that book? Something that had always been waiting for me to find?

No. I was overthinking it.
But deep in my chest, an inexplicable feeling whispered otherwise.

I couldn't concentrate on my work—no matter how hard I tried. My mind was consumed with thoughts of Shiuli, Poppy, and me. Something inside me whispered that Poppy was involved in all of this too, in ways I couldn't yet comprehend.

Just then, my phone lit up with a notification. Shiuli had sent me a follow request on Instagram. Excitedly, I accepted, and almost immediately, she messaged me about a picture I had posted of Poppy—completely coincidentally!

I told her all about Poppy, his quirks, his favourite treats, and how much he meant to me. In response, she told me the name of her own dog, named Puppy. I smiled at the coincidence.

Curious, I politely asked if she could send me a picture of Puppy with her. Moments later, my phone buzzed with another message.

I opened the picture, and my entire world shook.

Puppy looked almost identical to my Poppy! And also the name!

"This is all just a coincidence... right?" I whispered to myself, almost as if expecting an answer from within. But silence was all I got. No divine sign, no sudden realization—just the quiet hum of my thoughts. I sighed, letting the weight of uncertainty settle over me.

But one thing was certain—I wanted to meet her. I wanted to see Shiuli in person, to look into her eyes and confirm if this strange pull between us was real. More than that, I wanted to meet Puppy, to see if the resemblance to Poppy was as uncanny in reality as it seemed in pictures.

Most of all, I wanted to step into her world, to breathe in her presence, to drown in everything that was her.

I needed to meet her. **I needed to meet Puppy.**

I longed to pet Puppy, to run my fingers through his fur and see if he was as playful, as cheerful, as full of life as my Poppy had been. Would he wag his tail the same way? Would he look at me with the same mischievous sparkle in his eyes?

But an unsettling thought lingered in my mind—was it even possible? Could my Poppy, in some unfathomable way, now be her Puppy? Was fate playing an elaborate game, weaving our lives together in ways I couldn't yet comprehend?

I interrogated myself, searching for logic, for reason, but all I found was an inexplicable pull, a strange certainty that refused to leave my heart.

Back at my office, there was a girl who had fallen for me—deeply, unmistakably. I could see it in the way she looked at me, the way her eyes lingered just a second too long, the way she found reasons to strike up conversations. But my heart belonged elsewhere. I couldn't return her feelings, yet I wasn't the kind to be harsh or dismissive. I had to be careful with her emotions, handle them delicately. So, I crafted gentle excuses, weaving small, harmless stories—anything to subtly let her know that my heart was already spoken for, without breaking hers in the process.

But she never understood. She mistook my sincerity for hesitation, believing that I just needed time to consider *us*.

Her hope lingered in the spaces between our conversations, in the way she kept waiting for a different answer—one I could never give.

I didn't have the heart to shatter her feelings outright, yet I couldn't let the illusion continue either. So, I chose silence where words might mislead, distance where closeness might deceive. I carefully maintained the space between us, hoping she would one day see the truth—that my heart had already found its home *elsewhere*.

That day, she approached me with an excited gleam in her eyes, her voice bubbling with anticipation.

"**My parents want me to get married**," she said, then hesitated before adding, "**but... you know I have feelings for you, right?**"

I stood there, speechless. My mind was elsewhere—lost in the thought of *her*, of my Shiuli, of the undeniable connection that had consumed me. The weight of her words barely registered until she reached out, gently taking my hand as if she could read the turmoil on my face. Her grip was warm, searching—seeking understanding where I had none to give.

It was too much. Too close.

I pulled my hand away, my heart hammering in my chest. "**I'm in love with someone else**," I confessed, my voice steady but firm. "**My heart already belongs to the one fate has chosen for me.**"

Her expression shifted in an instant—confusion melting into anger, betrayal flickering in her gaze. "You led me on," she whispered, her voice trembling, but not from sadness—**from anger.**

I took a step back, startled. "I never did—"

"You may not have said it, but you knew," she cut me off, her eyes burning into mine. "You knew what I felt and still let me keep hoping. Why? Because it was easier?"

Her words were a dagger, **sharp and unforgiving**. Had I truly been so careless? Had my silence hurt her more than a firm rejection would have?

She inhaled sharply and then, in a voice quieter yet far more haunting, she murmured, "**Don't be so sure about fate. What if she's not who you think she is?**"

A cold shiver ran down my spine.

I wanted to dismiss her words, to shake them off as the bitterness of rejected love. But something about the way she said it—**the certainty in her voice**—stayed with me long after she walked away.

She felt deceived, wounded, but there was nothing I could do. I had made my choice long before this moment. My heart had already found its rightful owner, and nothing could change that now.

A wave of guilt crashed over me, heavy and relentless. I could see the hurt in her eyes, the silent question—*why?*—hanging between us like an unspoken plea.

Was I to blame for her heartbreak? Maybe. But had I ever encouraged her feelings? No. I had kept my distance, never once leading her on, never once giving her false hope. And yet, I hadn't been entirely honest either. I had avoided confronting the truth, choosing silence over clarity, afraid that my words might shatter her.

But now, looking at her, I realized that my silence had hurt her just the same.

I sighed, running a hand through my hair, struggling to find the right words. **"I'm sorry,"** I said at last, my voice barely above a whisper. **"I never meant to hurt you. I just... I don't know what else to say."**

She stood there, her hands clenched at her sides, waiting for more. I inhaled deeply, forcing myself to meet her gaze. **"You deserve love—the kind that is certain, unwavering. If it's not me, then maybe it's someone else. Maybe... you should give your parents' choice a chance.**

Or find someone who will cherish you the way you deserve."

Her lips parted slightly, as if she wanted to argue, but then she just exhaled sharply and looked away. I knew I had broken something inside her, but this was the only truth I could offer. And for both our sakes, I hoped it was enough.

My mind was still adrift in the remnants of my conversation with Shiuli, her words lingering in my thoughts like an echo I couldn't shake. No matter how much I tried to focus on the moment, on the weight of the situation in front of me, my heart kept pulling me back to her—to the warmth of our texts, to the effortless way she understood me without me having to say much at all.

Desperate for an escape, I reached for my phone, my fingers moving almost instinctively. I hesitated for a moment, staring at the screen, before finally deciding to text her.

"Hey, How are doing?"

It wasn't just an excuse to get away from the storm of emotions swirling around me—it was something more. I wanted to talk to her, to feel her presence through the small digital world. Maybe, just maybe, it would soothe the restless chaos in my chest.

I wanted to ask her for a voice note, to hear her voice, to feel her presence through something more than just words on a screen. But before I could even type out my request, my phone buzzed. A new message.

It was a **voice note**. From her.

I blinked in disbelief, my fingers frozen above the keyboard. Had she somehow read my mind? Was this just a coincidence, or was it something more—something beyond logic, beyond explanation?

My heart pounded as I stared at the message. A strange feeling crept over me, a mix of awe and curiosity. I hesitated, my thumb hovering over the play button. Why did I feel like this? **Why did hearing her voice feel like stepping into something irreversible?**
A lump formed in my throat. I had texted her, laughed with her, imagined her—but hearing her would be different. It would make her **real** in a way I wasn't sure I was ready for.
Would her voice be soft, like the way her words felt? Would it hold the same **familiarity that her presence in my life did, as if we had always known each other?**
I closed my eyes for a brief second and finally pressed play...

CHAPTER TEN

Her voice was beyond explanation—ethereal, almost divine. No words could truly capture what I felt in that moment. It wasn't just a voice; it was a melody, a whisper of something ancient and sacred. A part of me refused to believe that she was merely human.

No, she wasn't just Shiuli.

She was **Radha herself**. My Madhumohana's Radha.

I struggled to find the right words to praise her voice, but no matter how hard I tried, every word felt inadequate—too small, too ordinary to capture the divinity in her tone. It wasn't just a voice; it was an enchantment, a celestial hymn that stirred something deep within me.

She was Radha—pure, eternal, and divine.

I closed my eyes, and for a fleeting second, a vision surfaced—of another time, another world. A moonlit night. A melody in the air. A pair of anklets tinkling softly as she walked toward me, her silhouette merging with the fragrance of jasmine.

Had I met her before? Had I loved her long before this life had even begun?

I must have replayed her voice note at least twenty times, each listen making me more addicted to the melody of her voice. My thumb hovered over the play button. A ridiculous hesitation gripped me—why was I nervous?

It was just a voice note. Just sound.

And yet, deep inside, I knew it wasn't *just* that. The moment I heard her voice, something had shifted. Something irreversible.

Once was simply not enough—it never would be. Every word, every pause, every breath she took in that recording felt like a spell binding me to her.

It took me a good ten minutes to craft a response, lost in the trance she had unknowingly cast upon me. But before I could even hit send, another voice note arrived—one that felt like it had the power to pull me into another universe.

Smiling to myself, I finally replied, telling her that her voice was so mesmerizing it deserved to be my ringtone. To my surprise, she responded by sharing something even more precious—a song. A song she had sung herself.

I could hardly believe it. She had a voice that wasn't just meant to be heard but worshipped.

I couldn't quite put my finger on what exactly drew me to her, what tethered my soul so deeply to hers. Was it her voice? Her kindness? The way she always seemed to know what I needed before I even spoke a word?

Everything about her felt divine, as if she weren't just a person but a force—something beyond the ordinary, beyond the explainable. She wasn't just someone I liked; she was someone my heart had already chosen, someone my soul recognized even before my mind could comprehend it.

She wasn't just a passing presence in my life—she was the destination my heart had been searching for all along.

As soon as I wrapped up my work for the day, I rushed out of the office without letting a single stray thought cross my mind. My only focus was getting home as quickly as possible. I sped through the streets, the wind rushing

past me, my heart still racing with thoughts of Shiuli.
When I finally reached home, I was greeted by the sight of my sister and her husband, who had come over for a visit. The moment my sister looked at me, I knew I was caught. She had an uncanny ability to read my emotions just by glancing at my face, and this time was no exception.

I didn't spill everything to her, but she wasn't fooled. Her eyes sparkled with curiosity, and I could tell she had already sensed that something—something big—was going on in my life.

She kept throwing wild guesses at me, trying to piece together whatever secret I was hiding. Her excitement was contagious, and despite my best efforts to dodge her questions, she was relentless.

Then, out of nowhere, she smirked and asked, **"Did you find someone?"**

My breath hitched. Not because of her question—**but because, for the first time, my heart had an answer before I could deny it.**

Yes. I had found someone. (I whispered to myself)

But had I truly found her? Or had she always been waiting, hidden somewhere in the threads of fate, just waiting for me to remember her?

The moment those words left her lips, I felt my face heat up. A deep blush crept onto my cheeks, so intense that even a blind person could have sensed the emotions bubbling inside me. I tried to play it cool, but my sister wasn't fooled. She gasped dramatically, clapping her hands together.

"Oh my God, you did!" she squealed.

I groaned, burying my face in my palms, but deep down, I knew there was no escaping this conversation.

I quickly excused myself from my sister's relentless teasing and retreated to the comfort of my room. Without wasting a moment, I picked up my phone and texted my Radha.

To my delight, she had already replied. But this time, something felt different—she was opening up to me.

She confessed that it had been a long time since she felt this comfortable talking to someone. With every message, she revealed bits and pieces of her thoughts, her fears, and her dreams. It wasn't just small talk; it was something deeper, something real.

As I read her words, I could sense an invisible thread weaving between us, pulling us closer. It was as if the universe had aligned our souls in perfect harmony, creating a connection that felt both effortless and undeniable.

She shared something with me that I knew I would never be able to erase from my mind—something so profound that it shook me to my core.

In a hushed, almost sacred confession, she revealed a secret about her life. A truth so surreal that I found myself holding my breath as I read her words.

She told me that she could see Jagannath, the Lord of the Universe.

Jagannath—another form of my beloved Madhumohana.

A wave of emotion surged through me. Jagannath had always been a deity worshipped predominantly in the eastern lands of India, in Odisha. And though I was from Kerala, it had always been my silent dream to visit him, to stand before him at the grand temple in Puri and feel his divine presence.

And here she was—Shiuli—telling me that she didn't just dream of him; she saw him. My eyes froze on the screen. My breathing slowed. For a moment, I forgot how to exist.

Did I read that correctly?

She didn't just believe in Jagannath. She *saw* him.

She wasn't just a devotee; she was in love with him.

Her next words left me breathless.

She wanted to marry him...

I wasn't heartbroken—no, that wasn't the emotion consuming me. Instead, I was astonished, captivated by the depth of her devotion. How could someone love a deity so profoundly that they could see him, speak to him, and even yearn to marry him?

A part of me struggled to comprehend it, yet another part admired her unwavering faith. I had never encountered anyone like her before. Her love for Jagannath was not just faith—it was devotion in its purest form.

Could my love ever measure up to something so divine? A small, irrational fear crept into my heart—was there room for me in a heart already given to a god?

But I knew one thing for certain—we both shared the same love for Kanha.

Determined to find common ground between us, I told her something I had never voiced aloud. I confessed how, during my moments of deepest sorrow, whenever I had gone crying before Kanha, I had always seen a child. A divine, playful little boy who would appear in my mind, comforting me, making my burdens feel lighter. I had never truly understood what it meant, but it had always been real to me.

Shiuli listened with an intensity that made me feel as if, in that moment, I was the only person in existence. She didn't question, she didn't doubt—she simply absorbed every word, as if it was the most natural thing in the world. And that was when I made a silent promise to myself. I was determined.

Determined to make her fall in love with me just as deeply as I had fallen for her.

I was utterly captivated by her humility, her boundless gratitude, and the way she carried the weight of the world with such grace. Nothing else in existence could pull me in the way she did. Shiuli wasn't just someone I had met—she had become my everything.

It happened in the quietest of moments. A pause in our conversation, the way her voice softened as she spoke my name, the way she listened—truly listened—to every unspoken thought in me.

In that moment, something in me surrendered.

We talked endlessly, day and night, lost in a rhythm that felt timeless. Conversations stretched until dawn, yet neither of us ever seemed to have enough. We exchanged our birthdays, and to my surprise, she was truly stunned when she heard mine.

"My lucky number is 13," she said, almost as if the universe had conspired in our favour.

I chuckled, shaking my head in disbelief. "And my power number? It's your birthdate—9." I typed.

A coincidence? Maybe. But to us, it felt like destiny weaving its delicate thread between us, binding us closer than ever.

We became inseparable. I was completely, utterly obsessed.

Shiuli was more than just kind; she was an embodiment of warmth and compassion, a beacon of light that always seemed to find me in my darkest hours. She was the type of person who made the world feel softer, who reminded me what home truly felt like.

All my anguish, every struggle, every fleeting moment of pain—it all melted away the second I heard her sweet laughter. The way she spoke, the gentle cadence of her chocolaty voice, wrapped around me like a lullaby, soothing every restless storm inside me.

And just like that, I knew—there was no turning back.

She felt the same pull, the same inexplicable connection that bound us together. And then, as if voicing the thoughts lingering in both our hearts, she asked softly, "Do you believe in soulmates?"

I didn't even need to think. I was convinced—*she* was my soulmate. No one else could ever make me feel the way she did. No one else was *her*.

Without hesitation, I confessed my flourishing love for her, every emotion pouring out of me like a river breaking free from its dam. I knew—deep in my soul—that she felt it too. I could sense it in the pauses between her words, in the way she lingered before responding.

But then, her reply came, gentle yet measured. "*I need some days.*"

A pang of realization hit me. Had I rushed things? Had I overwhelmed her with the intensity of what I felt? I immediately apologized, fearing I had somehow broken the delicate harmony between us.

But she stopped me before I could spiral into doubt. With a voice so tender it felt like a caress, she said, "*No way, pretty guy! I have seen so much in life that my mind always rules over my heart when it comes to love.*"

Her words, her poise, the way she carried the weight of her past with such grace—*everything* about her was breath-taking. If this was a rejection, then it was the most beautiful one I had ever received.

But I wasn't ready to let go.

Not yet.

Not ever.

I gave her all the time she needed, waiting with the utmost purity in my heart for the moment she would accept my love. And when she finally did, it wasn't loud or dramatic—it was serene, like a quiet sunrise painting the world in golden hues. Her love was like the gentle waves of a river, flowing effortlessly into my life, filling every empty space with warmth and peace.

I was completely exhilarated. She wasn't just in my heart anymore—she was in my life.

One evening, as we were lost in one of our endless conversations, we found ourselves reminiscing about Poppy and Puppy. We laughed over their antics, the little things that made them special. Then, suddenly, she asked me a question that caught me completely off guard.

"Did your Poppy have any deformities?"

I froze. My heart skipped a beat.

He *did*.

My fingers slackened, nearly dropping my phone. The world around me blurred, the air in my lungs suddenly too thick to breathe. How could this be? It wasn't just a similarity—it was a message, a thread tying us together beyond time itself.

My mind raced with questions—how could she possibly know? It was something so specific, something I had never even mentioned to her. I conveyed my confusion, and what she told me next sent chills down my spine.

"My Puppy was born with the same deformity—a broken left leg."

For a moment, time stood still.

A realization hit me like a wave crashing onto the shore. It *wasn't* a coincidence. My Poppy *was* involved in this all along. Fate had been weaving its intricate threads long before I had even realized.

The revelation about Poppy and Puppy wasn't just a coincidence—it was something far beyond that. It was as if the universe had left behind a silent trail of breadcrumbs, leading me toward her, toward *us*. Their identical deformity, their uncanny resemblance—it wasn't ordinary. It felt like a celestial thread binding our souls long before we even knew of each other's existence.

But the most unsettling truth was yet to come. When I absentmindedly mentioned Poppy's death date, she fell silent for a moment. Then, in a voice laced with disbelief, she told me that it was the very same day her Puppy was born. A shiver ran down my spine. It was as if one soul had left my world only to enter hers, ensuring that the connection between us would never be severed.

This was no mere happenstance. It was as though Poppy, my childhood companion, had carried a piece of my destiny within him. And when he was gone, that missing piece of my heart had found its way to her—through Puppy—as if the universe itself had staged this delicate exchange.

It was as though Poppy's soul had travelled across time and space, ensuring that our destinies would one day intertwine.

Perhaps that was why, in the dim glow of my longing, I kept seeing Poppy's familiar form lingering with her silhouette. As if he was never truly gone, as if he had merely changed his vessel, **guiding me—always guiding me**—to *her*.

This was another undeniable connection between us, another whisper from the universe reminding me—she *was* my soul-mate.

CHAPTER TWELVE

We were both over the moon, feasting in the miracle of having found each other in a world so vast and chaotic. A year and a half had passed since our souls had intertwined, and now, it was time to bridge the distance that still lingered between us. The time had come to finally stand before each other, not just in words or whispers, but in reality.

Her voice echoed in my mind, a promise she had made countless times before— *"The day we meet, you will find yourself. Your truth, your identity—the very answer that has kept you restless since the day you first cried."*

I never truly understood what she meant, but now, with each heartbeat drawing me closer to that moment, I felt it. A shift in the air, a pull toward something inevitable, something profound.

She told me she was traveling to Kerala—Kochi, to be precise—and saying that I was excited would be the greatest understatement of my life. My heart pounded with a rhythm I had never known before, a mix of nervous anticipation and sheer exhilaration.

I had prepared everything just the way she would love it. No roses—she always preferred jasmine and orchids, their fragrance delicate and enchanting, just like her presence in my life. I held them tightly, as if they were carrying a piece of my love.

Any moment now, she would land on my soil, step into my reality. And for the first time, I would see her—not through the glow of a screen, not through the sound of a voice note, but right before me, in all her divinity. I had imagined this moment a thousand times—her face, her touch, the way the world would fade the moment she stepped into my arms. And yet, standing there, I realized nothing could have prepared me for the weight of reality pressing against my chest.

My princess was finally coming home—to me.

And then, the moment I had been waiting for arrived. My phone buzzed, and her name flashed on the screen. I took a deep breath before answering.

"I'm here," she said, her voice laced with excitement and warmth.

Her plane had landed. Any second now, she would step into my world—not as a distant dream, not as a voice in the wind, but as a tangible reality.

My heart pounded furiously, an erratic rhythm of longing and nervous anticipation. My palms were slightly damp, my breath uneven. The weight of the moment pressed down on me, yet I welcomed it. I was about to meet the woman who had unknowingly rewritten my destiny.

And the truth was—I had no idea what was about to hit me.

The world around me faded into a blur of meaningless motion as the airport doors slid open. And then, there she was—standing amidst the crowd, her eyes searching for me. The moment our gazes met, time slowed, and everything else ceased to exist. The chaos of the airport melted away. The overhead announcements, the hurried footsteps, the beeping of baggage carts—all of it blurred into silence. All I could hear was the invisible tether between us tightening, pulling me toward the only thing that had ever truly mattered.

Shiuli.

She was draped in simplicity yet carried an ethereal glow that made my breath hitch. The soft curls of her hair danced slightly with the breeze, and her doe-like eyes held a universe I longed to explore. A hesitant yet knowing smile graced her lips, and in that instant, I felt myself falling in love all over again—deeper, harder, and more irrevocably than before.

My feet felt glued to the ground, my heart hammering as if trying to reach her before I could. She took a small step forward, and as if pulled by an unseen force, so did I. Each step toward her felt like walking into a long-lost dream, one I had lived a thousand times in my mind but was only now getting to touch.

And then, I was standing right before her, close enough to see the flicker of emotion in her eyes—the same emotion that was flooding through me.

"You're real" I whispered, almost in disbelief.

She laughed softly, that melodious sound wrapping around me like a warm embrace.

As she stepped closer, my breath caught in my throat. That was when I truly noticed—she was wearing white. The very colour I had always wished to see her in. It wasn't just a coincidence; it felt as if the universe had conspired to paint this moment exactly as I had dreamed. The soft fabric of her dress flowed gracefully with every step, mirroring the quiet elegance she carried within her.

And her face—oh, her face! It was glowing with an unknown happiness, a radiance that outshone even the golden sun that poured through the airport glass. Her eyes shimmered with something indescribable, as if she, too, had been waiting for this very moment her entire life.

I stood frozen, drinking in every detail, memorizing the way she moved, the way her lips curled into the most delicate, heart-stopping smile. My world had just aligned with hers, and I knew, without a sliver of doubt, that this was the beginning of something eternal. Yet, in the depths of my soul, a whisper of unease stirred. Love as profound as this often came with a price. And in that moment, I feared the universe would one day demand its due.

I instinctively leaned in for a hug, my heart eager to finally hold her, but she took a step back, raising her hand with a playful glint in her eyes.

"Stop! Not yet, my pretty guy," she teased, her voice laced with mischief.

If it had been anyone else, I might have been taken aback, maybe even a little offended. But because it was her—because it was *Shiuli*—I simply smiled. She had this way of making even the simplest moments feel special, of turning ordinary gestures into something profound.

She tilted her head slightly, her eyes locking onto mine. "Take me to your favourite spot," she said, her tone gentle yet certain.

There was no hesitation, no need for questions. I already knew where I had to take her. That one place that held pieces of my heart, the very place I had once captured in a photograph, unknowingly saving it for *this* day.

With a silent nod, I extended my hand, and though she didn't take it yet, she followed me without a second thought. My princess had arrived, and I was about to show her the world through my eyes.

As we arrived, she stepped out of the car with a quiet certainty, as if she had been here before—as if every stone, every whispering leaf, every breath of this place already belonged to her.

I watched in silent awe as she moved, not with hesitation, but with an unshakable knowing. She didn't ask me where to go. She didn't need to. Her feet carried her effortlessly, straight to *that* spot—the very place where I had last seen my Poppy.

My breath hitched. How did she know? How was she so inevitable in everything she did?

I followed her, unable to do anything else. The distance between us stretched and shrank with the rhythm of the wind, and there, standing in the golden embrace of the evening sun, she became ethereal. The gentle breeze played with her hair, lifting soft strands that danced around her face, and in that moment, she turned to me.

Her eyes held something beyond time, beyond understanding—a gaze that felt like a doorway to a truth I had never dared to see.

And then, she asked, her voice carrying the weight of something far greater than just words.

"Ready to see the reality, my pretty guy?"

I didn't utter a word. Words felt meaningless in the presence of something far greater—something I couldn't yet comprehend.

Without hesitation, I walked straight to her, drawn by an invisible force stronger than logic, stronger than reason.

As soon as she took my hand, a jolt shot through me—*a literal shock*! My breath hitched, my skin tingled, and for a brief moment, it felt as if the universe itself had surged through my veins. It wasn't painful, but it wasn't ordinary either. It was a spark, a pulse of something ancient and unknown.

Her grip remained firm, unwavering, as if she had expected this. As if she knew exactly what was happening. And I—*I could only look at her, mesmerized, shaken, and completely hers.*

Her fingers grazed the "*S*" mark on my hand, and in that instant, reality as I knew it shattered.

A force surged through me, beyond time, beyond existence—pulling me into something unfathomable, something infinite. It felt like the universe was rewiring itself inside me. My past and future collided in a single pulse, a silent explosion of everything I had ever been and everything I was yet to become. I wasn't just witnessing truth—I was unravelling into it.

My breath left me, my vision blurred, and my body trembled as an overwhelming truth unfolded before my very eyes.

I saw—**myself**.

Not just as a man standing in that moment, but as something far greater. **I was the beginning and the end.** I was the vast, endless sky stretching beyond comprehension. I was the first whisper of the wind and the last echo of a dying star. I was the birth of light and the womb of darkness. **I was the universe itself.** I helped people, I was the creator and the destroyer! **I was everything I had been searching for!**

And she—she had always been there.

In every moment. In every lifetime.

I saw her face in flickering flashes—sometimes as a distant gaze across a crowded marketplace, sometimes as a lingering presence beside me in the quietest of nights. Sometimes as a lover, sometimes as a stranger passing by.

But always there.

Always.

She was the golden thread woven through the fabric of my existence. The silent rhythm in the song of my soul. The shadow that walked beside me in every life, every universe, every breath I had ever taken.
And yet, I had never known.
Pain swelled in my chest, a raw, unbearable ache. **How could I have been so blind?** How could I have spent lifetimes searching for something that had always been right beside me?
This is the exact experience that I had felt when the silhouette came and pressed the 's' mark on my hand. It was her, always! And it will be her forever!
Tears blurred my vision, but through them, I saw her.
My Shiuli. My Radha. My eternal one.
She held my hand firmly, grounding me, as if she knew—**as if she had always known**.
"I told you, my pretty guy," she whispered, her voice as soft as the breeze yet as powerful as the storm raging within me. *"The day we met, you would find yourself."*
I gasped for air, my knees threatening to give way. **I was nothing, yet I was everything.** I was shattered, yet I had never been more whole.
My fingers curled around hers, desperate, needing, aching.
"Don't let go," I choked, my voice barely above a whisper.
She smiled—the saddest, most beautiful smile I had ever seen.
"I never have," she said. "And I never will."
And in that moment, I *knew*—even if the universe collapsed, even if time itself unravelled, even if every star turned to dust—*she would find me again.*
In another life.

In another universe.
In another breath.
And I—*I would wait for her, in every single one of them.*
It's been 30 years that I met her and today is the day
she left for the heaven's abode.

I sit here, alone, with a weight so heavy on my chest
that even breathing feels like a betrayal. The silence is the
hardest part. It isn't just the absence of her voice—it's the
absence of the world as I once knew it. Colours seem
duller, time stretches endlessly, and every breath feels like
an echo of the one I once shared with her.

My hands tremble as I write, my vision blurred by the
storm that refuses to quiet within me. Every letter I carve
onto this paper feels like a wound reopening, every word
an echo of her laughter that now only exists in the silence.

She is gone.

Gone, and yet, she is everywhere. In the whisper of the
wind, in the fragrance of jasmine, in the hush of the night
that once carried her voice to me. She was my reality, my
truth, my home. And now, I am a house without walls, a
traveller without a destination.

But I write. I write because I need to tell you
something, something she made me see when she was
here, something that cannot die even if she has.

Your soul has its mate—somewhere out there. Maybe in
this life, maybe in another, but it exists. And when you
find them, you will know. Not because of the way they
look at you, not because of the words they say, but because
of the way they fit within your existence, like they have
always belonged there.

I know this now.

I know this because I found mine. And though she is no
longer here to hold my hand, to call me her 'pretty guy,' I

know she still walks with me, just as she always has. In every life. In every universe.

If you dare to question everything, if you break free from what you have been told and listen—truly listen—to the ache inside you, you will find your way. And when you do, hold onto them. Hold onto them like they are the only truth in this fleeting world.

Because one day, they will leave. And when that day comes, you will wish you had just one more moment. One more breath. One more chance to tell them that they were your beginning and your end.

Just like she was mine.

Afterword

Every story is more than just words on a page—it is a journey, both for the writer and the reader. Writing The Mark That Led Me to You has been an exploration of mystery, fate, and self-discovery, and I hope it has resonated with you in some way.

Thank you for stepping into this world and following the mark. I would love to hear your thoughts and experiences—how this book made you feel, what questions it left you with, and what meaning you found within its pages.

Stories have a way of bringing people together, and I am grateful that this one has connected us.

Author's Note

The idea for this book came from my deep curiosity about the unseen forces that shape our lives. Whether we call it fate, intuition, or coincidence, there are moments that feel like they are guiding us toward something greater.

Through this novel, I wanted to explore the power of signs, forgotten truths, and the choices we make in pursuit of understanding. While the story itself is fictional, its essence—the search for meaning—is something I believe we all experience in our own ways.

Thank you for reading, for questioning, and for embarking on this journey with me.

About The Author

SHEPHALI HAZRA

Shephali Hazra, an English Honours graduate, has always been guided by curiosity and creativity. Drawn to both mystery and spirituality, she blends these elements in her storytelling, creating narratives that intrigue and inspire.

A dedicated learner, Shephali has always valued education and personal growth. Beyond her love for literature, she nurtures a deep-seated ambition of becoming an IAS officer, a goal that reflects her perseverance and commitment to making a difference. When she's not writing, she finds joy in singing, a hobby that allows her to express herself in another beautiful way.

"The Mark That Led Me to You" is a heartfelt attempt to bring together her love for storytelling, introspection, and the unknown. Through this book, she hopes to take readers on a journey of discovery—one that resonates long after the final page is turned.